Little House HOTEL

John Sandford

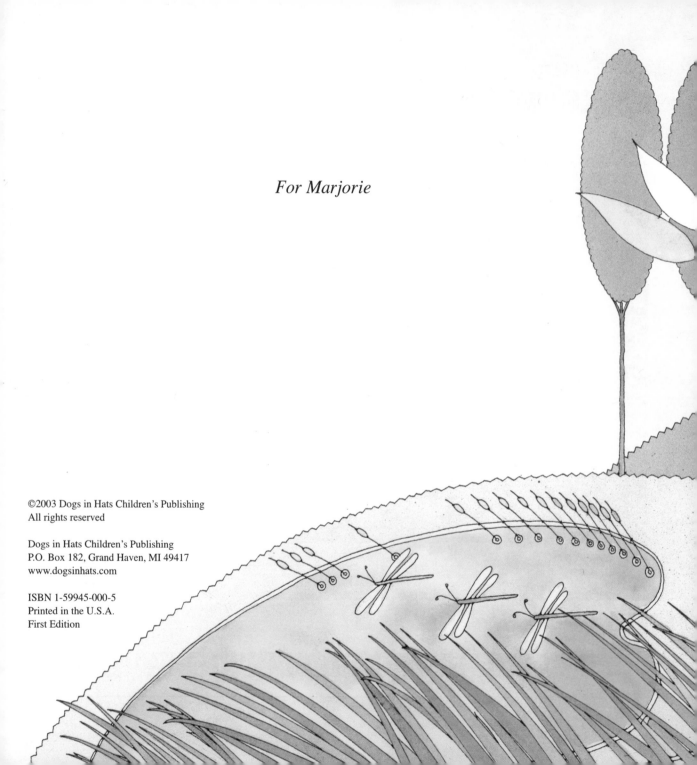

For Marjorie

Dogs in Hats Children's Publishing
P.O. Box 182, Grand Haven, MI 49417
www.dogsinhats.com

ISBN 1-59945-000-5
Printed in the U.S.A.
First Edition

Marjorie Butterfly had been meaning
to get around to her spring cleaning.
"I'll scrub my little house so well
and open Little House Hotel."

She had much to clear away,
the guests were due to come *today!*
She used elbow grease for polishing doors,
washing dishes and sweeping floors.

Guest Number One, Kaskaskia Phrog
bowed, tipped his hat, and signed the inn's log.
He was on his way to the South Caribbean -
a good place to go if you're amphibian.

Bellflower Mouse was guest Number Two.
She curtsied and whispered, "How do you do?"
Marjorie gave a butterfly grin.
"Welcome, Bellflower, to my very small inn."

Guest Number Three came all in a hurry.
His feet, tail, and ears were all big and furry.
"I can pay for two nights, look here, take my money!"
He signed the register Cahokia Bunny.

Announcing his presence, guest Number Four
ordered that someone hold open the door.
"Put chocolates on pillow, fine soap with soft towel!"
Oglesby Rooster was a most demanding fowl.

Though some called it breakfast and some called it lunch,
they all enjoyed dear Marjorie's brunch.
The odd group got on remarkably well -
such is the magic of Little House Hotel.

Marjorie soaked in her *Flutterbye® Bubbles*
unaware of nearby weatherish troubles.
While others played cards, Phrog read his Twain,
the sky grew darker and it started to rain.

What a whopper of a storm! What lightning! What hail!
It was weather best suited to catfish or whale.
Approaching the doorstep, so late to arrive,
was McNabb the Bear - guest Number Five.

"Please give me a room! I'm wet and I'm cold.
I'll pay you in honey, or coupons, or gold!
Please give me a room, that's all I that I ask.
I'll help you by doing any difficult task."

Said Marjorie after a *flash* and a BOOM,
"I'm so sorry Bear, we just don't have the room!
Climb up to the chimney to sit out the storm.
You'll still be wet, but at least you'll be warm."

"I certainly hope this isn't a *goof*,"
He thought as he made his way to the roof.
"Just try to stay warm, and wait out the weather,"
said Bear as he rubbed his big paws together.

He warmed frozen elbows, knees, feet and toes,
yawned a big *yawn* and started to doze.
He was just getting comfy taking his naps..
..when the hotel gave way - *into total collapse!*

They looked all around – how could it be possible?
All that remained was entirely tossable!
"You can help clear it up, this big pile of slush.
We'll give it a big, gigantical flush!"

"I'm so embarrassed - *I am,* I confess!
I'll do what I can to help with this mess.
But when garbage is emptied and dumpsters are filled,
I'll design your new hotel – and then start to build.

Bear built a hotel that was higher and longer
deeper and wider and bigger and stronger!
Everyone helped to turn the destruction
into a true wonder of modern construction.

These days they're all happy,
the inn runs swell —
and there's room for *all guests*
at the *Big* House Hotel.